Just at Daylight . . .

"Here mousy, mousy, mousy," said the little girl. It was Tatty. She had gotten up before anyone else was awake. She had saved a small piece of bread from her supper the night before, and she sat on the stairs crumbling it and tossing the crumbs down the steps to a bare spot on the cellar floor.

"Here mousy, mousy," she called again softly.

Mother Mouse watched with considerable surprise. She had never seen anyone doing anything like this before. She did not move a whisker or even the tip of her tail.

Then at last, with a sigh, Tatty stood up and went back up the stairs. When everything had been quiet for a while, Mother Mouse came down and tasted the bread crumbs. They were real bread crumbs all right; very fresh and tasty. Mother Mouse hurried to wake up Violet and Baby Mouse, who were sleepy, but not too sleepy to eat. It had been two days since they had had any food.

THE
GOOD DAY
MICE

by Carol Beach York

Illustrated by Victoria de Larrea

A BANTAM SKYLARK BOOK®
TORONTO · NEW YORK · LONDON · SYDNEY · AUCKLAND

For my editor, Corinne Naden,
because she likes my stories

RL 3, 008–011

THE GOOD DAY MICE
*A Bantam Book / published by arrangement with
the Author*

PRINTING HISTORY
*First published in the United States by Franklin Watts, Inc.,
of New York.*
Bantam Skylark edition / February 1986

ISBN 0-553-15373-0

Published simultaneously in the United States and Canada

---

*Bantam Books are published by Bantam Books, Inc. Its trade-
mark, consisting of the words "Bantam Books" and the por-
trayal of a rooster, is Registered in U.S. Patent and Trademark
Office and in other countries. Marca Registrada. Bantam
Books, Inc., 666 Fifth Avenue, New York, New York 10103.*

PRINTED IN THE UNITED STATES OF AMERICA

CW   0 9 8 7 6 5 4 3 2 1

Contents

1

The Mouse Family

Autumn had come to Butterfield Square. Fallen leaves lay along the curb. Around the Square all the brick houses stood in a row, just as they had stood for so many autumns before. The red bricks on some houses were fading, but the stone steps were swept clean and the knockers on the heavy old doors were polished brightly.

At Number 18 Butterfield Square, *The Good Day Orphanage for Girls,* dry leaves rattled against iron fence rails glistening with a fresh coat of black paint. The handyman wiped his hands on a red handkerchief and gathered up his paint bucket and brush. Daylight was ending; he had just finished in time.

As the handyman shuffled away across the side yard toward the cellar doorway, around the corner and up the street came a small brown mouse family.

"Wet paint, wet paint," Father Mouse warned, even before the mouse family had come far enough along the fence to see the sign that the handyman had left: WET PAINT.

"Careful now, my dears, careful." Father Mouse turned his sleek fat little brown head to speak over his shoulder to Mother Mouse and Baby Mouse, who came close behind him.

Baby Mouse was no bigger than one of the tiny brown leaves that lay curled on the ground. In fact, he often scampered under a leaf by mistake, thinking that was the way to go. So Mother Mouse stayed close beside him, and Father Mouse led the way ahead.

Last of all came Violet Mouse, scurrying to keep up because she did not want to become lost in a strange place.

2

"This is it! This is it!" Father Mouse cried suddenly with great excitement. He had just caught sight of the name "Butterfield Square" on the street sign. "Look, my dear," he called to Mother Mouse. "We have found Butterfield Square!"

"Oh, at last!" Mother Mouse said gratefully. Then they all stood still as mice and looked around uncertainly.

The street was very quiet. It was dusky now, and there were lights in some of the houses around the Square. Night was coming.

"We must find some place for the night," Mother Mouse said.

Violet Mouse wriggled her smooth tiny mouse nose and said, "Yes, I'm tired—and I'm hungry, too. And it's getting cold."

Baby Mouse did not say anything. He had fallen asleep under a leaf.

Father Mouse took charge at once. "We'll all be cold if we don't get in somewhere," he said. Although the days were still warm and sunny and full of soft haze and the tangy smell of burning leaves, it was true that the nights were quite chilly. For that is the way autumn is.

"What's wrong with this place right here?" Father Mouse asked. "What more could we ask for?" He grandly flourished a paw toward Number 18, as though he himself had specially ordered the large brick house that they were standing in front of, its yard circled neatly by the freshly painted black iron fence.

"It does look cozy," Mother Mouse said. There were lights on in the house, upstairs and down, and it looked very cheerful in the twilight.

Father Mouse went first. Mother Mouse poked Baby Mouse to wake him up, and they both followed Father Mouse. Violet shivered and hurried after. She did not want to be left alone in the strange street. She wished that she were safe at home, sleeping on the nice piece of red carpet they had in their own cellar.

Through the fence ran the mice, across the grass and crunchy leaves. They followed the same way that the handyman had walked, and soon found themselves beside the cellar door at the side of the house near the back. It was a slanting wooden door that came right down to the ground, and a stone had caught in the corner so that the door was not closed all the way. No one was in sight, and one by one the little brown mice slipped through the open corner at the bottom of the door and ran down the flight of steps below, into the warm dark cellar. Even Violet began to feel somewhat better—although she was sure that this was not going to be as nice as their cellar at home. She was certain there would be no warm piece of red carpet to sleep upon, no lovely carpet fringe to play with and chew on.

"Over here, over here," called Father Mouse. "Here's just the place for us."

Mother Mouse and Baby Mouse and Violet hurried along after him, past the garden tools and the coal bin and the laundry tubs. Inside the cellar was another flight of stairs, narrow wooden ones with a wooden handrail. These stairs led up to a door—a kitchen door, the mouse family were all sure, for that was where cellar stairs usually led. This door was closed, but a line of light shone at the bottom, and they

could smell some very tasty things cooking. Violet began to feel even better. Maybe they could get something to eat now. She was sure that it must be long past suppertime.

"Here we go, here we go," Father Mouse said, and he led his family under the wooden stairs, where an old bushel basket had rolled over on its side. Clean soft rags spilled out across the floor.

"Who could ask for anything better than this? Not even a king!" Father Mouse declared.

"Who could ask for anything better than this," Mother Mouse agreed. She was trying to sound cheerful, too; but they were all so weary. They had traveled all day, since before light that morning. They had come such a long way.

"Who could ask for anything better than this?" said Baby Mouse. He liked to say what everyone else said.

I could ask for my red carpet, Violet Mouse thought to herself, but she did not say anything. Suddenly she was too tired to care what she slept on. She flopped down on a pile of soft rags at the back of the bushel basket, curled her tail around her, put her head daintily down upon her paws, and went to sleep. Baby Mouse snuggled beside her and went to sleep, too.

But Mother and Father Mouse did not go to sleep. They had come on a very, very important errand, and they must now make further plans.

"I will begin tomorrow as soon as it is light," Father Mouse said. "We have found Butterfield Square. I am sure that is a good sign."

2

What Happened to Frederick

The mouse family's real home was far away across the city in the cellar of a big comfortable frame house. The house had a front yard with plenty of rose bushes for the mice to play under. Of course, a family of people lived in the rooms of the house. The mice had their home downstairs under some boxes by the furnace. A piece of red carpet, set aside by the owners because it was wearing thin in the middle, was Violet's favorite thing. An old wool sweater worn out at the elbows made a lovely bed for Mother and Father Mouse and Baby Mouse—and Frederick Mouse, who was not so very much bigger than Baby Mouse, but a good deal more lively and daring—which was what had caused all the trouble.

One day, not long before the mouse family journeyed to Butterfield Square, the people who lived upstairs in the house had company. The mice could hear visitors' voices and the tramp of feet and the creaking of floors in the living room and kitchen and dining room. Frederick Mouse wanted to run right upstairs and see the fun, but Mother Mouse said: "Certainly not!"

That was the *last* thing any of the mice should do.

But Frederick Mouse could hardly bear to stay down in the cellar and listen to all the noises above without going to see. Violet had found some thrown-away ribbons, and she dressed herself up with bows on her tail and around her neck. Baby Mouse chewed on the woolen sweater. Everyone was contented except Frederick, and finally Father Mouse said, oh, all right, he would take Frederick himself, just for one small peek upstairs.

Mother Mouse did not like it. She did not think it was safe. She did not think it was wise. Oh, why are men so adventurous? she worried to herself, shaking her head with disapproval as they brushed up their whiskers and set out.

Father Mouse and Frederick went up through the pantry hole that they had found long ago, and sure enough the pantry door was open, so they went right on into the kitchen. The people were having their dessert in the dining room, and all the other food had been brought back to the kitchen from the dining-room table. Oh, what a splendid sight that kitchen was! There were platters of ham and chicken, dishes of pickles and applesauce, and a large plate stacked high with slices of soft white bread. It made Father Mouse's mouth water just to see it all.

"I think if we take your mother a nice piece of that white bread, she will not think we were so foolish to come, after all," he said to Frederick.

The two mice were scampering across the kitchen floor when a man walked in from the dining room. He did not see Father Mouse, who was behind a chair leg, but he did see Frederick—and before the poor little mouse could get away, the man reached down and caught him up by the tail.

Just then a boy came into the kitchen, carrying his empty dessert plate. "What have you got, Daddy?" the boy cried. "A mouse! A mouse! Can I have him, Daddy? Can I have him for a pet?"

At the word "mouse" all the people came in from the dining room and stood around in the kitchen—although some of the ladies did not stand too close. All the children stared enviously at the boy who was going to have the mouse for a pet. Father Mouse shrank back behind the chair leg and watched with quivering rage to see his own dear Frederick dangling so high above him in the air.

"Help! Help!" shrieked Frederick. But it only sounded like a mouse squeak to the people. Then everyone went out of the kitchen,

taking Frederick Mouse with them, and although his cries grew fainter and fainter—
". . . help . . . help . . ."—each frantic cry
pierced Father Mouse to his very heart.

Father Mouse waited behind the chair in
the kitchen for a while, and then he crept carefully through the hallway of the house to see if
he could find where the people had taken Frederick. To his dismay he saw that the visitors
were preparing to leave. They stood clustered
around the front door, putting on their coats
and hats. The little boy who wanted to make a
pet out of Frederick was holding a small cardboard box with tiny holes punched in the top.

"Nice mouse," he was saying to the box.
Father Mouse shuddered, and hid behind the
umbrella rack.

At last everyone went outside, and in despair Father Mouse followed, running in the
grass by the walk, trying to keep out of sight. A
taxicab had drawn up at the curb, and as the
departing visitors climbed into the taxi, Father
Mouse heard the man who had caught Frederick by the tail tell the driver the name of the

street where they wished to go. Father Mouse did not hear distinctly what street it was, for the children were chattering away about who was going to sit by the windows. But then Father Mouse did hear the man add, "That's near Butterfield Square."

The taxicab door slammed shut and away went the visitors—with Frederick. The other people waved good-bye and then went back into the house.

Poor Father Mouse had stood alone at the curb, his little heart beating hard and his eyes filling with tears.

3

Twenty-eight Little Girls

Mother Mouse had not said "I told you so." She did not say "Now see what you have done." She had not scolded at all, because she could see that Father Mouse felt bad enough already. She had not even cried one tear. They had waited until morning so that Baby Mouse and Violet could have their night's rest, but before it was light they had all set off together to find Butterfield Square and whatever street was near it, and rescue Frederick.

Violet took off all her ribbons, for Mother

Mouse said she could not wear them on the trip.

It had been a long, weary day—running, asking directions when they could, which was not often, for they met hardly any other mice the whole day. Most mice stay safely out of sight when it is daylight and people are walking about in the streets. However, Father Mouse knew a few places where he roused up some old friends in their alley homes, and by and by, bit by bit, the mouse family found their way to Butterfield Square. They could see when they arrived that there were many streets around the Square. Streets went off at every corner in different directions. And some of the houses towered five and six stories high, full of rooms. How would it be possible to find the right street and then the right house and the right room, from so many. . . ? But even then Mother Mouse did not cry one tear.

When they were safely settled under the stairs in the strange cellar at Number 18, Mother and Father Mouse made their plans and kept watch while Baby Mouse and Violet slept. They listened to the sounds above and smelled the good supper smells coming from the kitchen. There seemed to be quite a lot of foot-steps coming and going, and the mice won-dered who lived in this big house. When everything had at last grown silent, Father Mouse went to see if he could find something for his family to eat. He returned with a piece of cake that he had found in the kitchen. Mother Mouse and Father Mouse ate some of the cake and saved some for their children to have when they woke up.

"I hope wherever he is that Frederick is having something good for his supper," said Father Mouse.

Mother Mouse was hoping that Frederick was having any supper at all, and that he wasn't hungry—or frightened or lonely or sad. "I hope Frederick is not too frightened," she said after a bit. "Do you think he will guess we are coming to rescue him?"

"I don't know," said Father Mouse. "I hope so . . . I hope that boy is kind to him." Father

Mouse's voice began to tremble and he did not talk anymore.

At last, very tired themselves, Mother Mouse and Father Mouse closed their eyes and went to sleep.

In the morning Baby Mouse and Violet were quite pleased to see cake for breakfast. Maybe it will not be so bad here, after all, Violet thought; and almost right away she caught sight of a paint can with a shiny side like a mirror, and she went over to admire herself.

Father Mouse was preparing to go out and begin his search among the strange streets and strange houses, when suddenly the mouse family began to hear voices and footsteps above. There seemed to be a great many voices and a great many footsteps. There were dishes and pans rattling in the kitchen, and sounds of many chairs moving up to the breakfast table.

"My," said Mother Mouse, "it must be a very large family that lives in this house."

Most of the voices sounded like children's voices to Mother and Father Mouse, and they were not sure they liked that very much. They

did not feel very friendly toward children, since a boy had taken off their own dear Frederick in a cardboard box.

"We will be very quiet," Father Mouse said to Mother Mouse. "They will never know we are here. Maybe there are not so many as we think."

But then, as Father Mouse was starting across the yard toward the black iron fence to begin his search for Frederick, the door of the house opened and out came the children. Little girls and more little girls, and *more* little girls. Father Mouse could hardly believe his own eyes. Twenty-seven little girls came out, all wearing the same dark blue coats and long black stockings and black shoes with buckles at the sides. They were carrying school books and shuffling their feet through the fallen leaves. Then, when Father Mouse was still not sure he could believe his eyes, one more little girl came out, calling, "Wait for me, wait for me," as she ran. *Twenty-eight little girls!*

Father Mouse did not know it, of course, but the house he had chosen was the home of

The Good Day Orphanage for Girls. Twenty-eight little girls.

When the children were all out of sight around the corner, Father Mouse, somewhat shaken, went on his way. Perhaps, he thought to himself, he would find another house suitable in which to stay. While he looked for his darling Frederick, he would also keep his eyes open for a house with not quite so many children.

But although he kept his eyes open all that morning and afternoon, Father Mouse did not find Frederick, and he did not find a house that seemed better than the one they already had.

When he returned to the cellar at Number 18 Butterfield Square just before dusk that afternoon, he said to Mother Mouse: "There are indeed a great many children in this house, but they are all girls, and that is not nearly so bad as boys, I'm sure. You wouldn't believe how many of the other houses have either a cat staring out of the window or a dog lounging around the front yard. At the house on the corner there is the biggest dog I have ever seen in my life, and at another house nearby there are six cats sleeping on the doorsill."

Mother Mouse said she thought they were perhaps as well off where they were, if that was the case.

4

Under the Stairs

Several days passed. Every morning Father Mouse would go out and explore another street. He would begin at the corner where the street met Butterfield Square. He would go up one side of the street for two or three blocks, and then he would cross the street and come back on the other side. He would run up on the porches of the houses and creep along windowsills and through any door that he could find ajar. He saw many kinds of houses and all kinds of people, and he had to be very careful to stay out of the way of any cats and dogs who were pets in the houses.

But he did not see Frederick anywhere. Nor did he see the man who had caught Frederick by the tail. And he did not see the boy who had wanted Frederick for his pet.

Sometimes Father Mouse would meet another mouse in the alleyway behind the houses.

"Say, have you heard of anybody around here having a pet mouse?" Father Mouse would ask. "Any boy in one of these houses?"

Why, no, the mice always said; they never had.

Father Mouse would be very tired and discouraged when it was time to go back to his family at the end of the day. But he put up a brave front. He knew how disappointed Mother Mouse would be to hear that there was no news, and he felt more and more at fault because he had been the one to take Frederick up into that kitchen when the company was there.

Mother Mouse always waited anxiously until Father Mouse returned. She was never sure if he was safe from cats and dogs. And she could not really relax in this strange house. She missed her own corner by the furnace in the cellar where she had been born. She missed the soft woolen sweater and the pretty red carpet and the familiar smell of things. But she did not say anything about this to anyone else. When Violet said, "When are we going to find Frederick and go home, Mama?" Mother Mouse would only reply, "We will be going home one of these days."

At dusk, when Father Mouse would come back and say that he had not found Frederick today but he surely would find him soon, Mother Mouse always said, "Yes, perhaps tomorrow you will find him."

Then after everyone else was asleep Mother Mouse would lie on the scraps in the back of the bushel basket and listen to the unfamiliar sounds of the unfamiliar house. Even after everyone upstairs had gone to bed, the house had sounds of its own to make. A board would creak, a shutter would thump, a clock would strike somewhere in the rooms upstairs. A tree branch scraped against a window, dry leave rustled down upon the roof. At home the sounds were much the same, sounds heard in any house when everyone has gone to bed. But they were not the same to Mother Mouse. She wanted to be home in her own cellar again, and she wanted all her family with her. Every single one. Frederick, too.

But she did not cry one tear.

Father Mouse was homesick, too, and he could not help but see that his little family grew more quiet and sad as each day passed. He tried to think of what he could do to cheer them up. One night when he had come home with still no news of Frederick, and even more tired than usual—for he had been chased that day by five different cats—his family was more quiet and sad than ever. He knew that he must do something. Although he was very weary and troubled himself, Father Mouse made his voice very gay.

"Tonight we are going to have a party!" he said.

"A party—a party—!" Violet and Baby Mouse clamored, anxious to begin.

"First, we have to have some good things to eat for our party," Father Mouse said. "Then we shall begin."

Father Mouse and Mother Mouse went up the stairs and peeked through the kitchen door, which was open just a crack. Cook was bustling about carrying dishes to the table in the dining room. Two little girls were helping her. They had long white aprons over their dark blue dresses. Mother and Father Mouse waited, and soon the table was all ready for supper. The little girls went to the dining room to eat with the others. Cook was the only one in the kitchen.

Mother and Father Mouse waited a little more, and Cook went into the dining room to see if there was anything else needed there. While she was out of the kitchen, quick as he could, Father Mouse scampered to a cupboard and took an oatmeal cookie that had been left behind. Mother Mouse went under the kitchen stove and took a fat purple grape that had rolled there.

Then they scurried back to the cellar door and were just safely out of sight when Cook came back into the kitchen.

"Now we can have our party," Father Mouse said. "First we will have some songs and recitations."

"Yes, yes," everyone agreed.

"Who wants to be first?" said Father Mouse. He would have liked to be first himself, but he was always polite.

"I'll be first," said Baby Mouse, and he began to sing: *"Sing a song of sixpence, a pocket full of pins . . ."*

"That's not right at all," Violet Mouse said with scorn. "If you don't know the right words, you shouldn't try to sing something."

Then she began to recite her verse:

"Little Miss Muffet
  Sat on a tuffet
  Eating her Christmas pie.
  Along came a beetle
  Sat down on a needle
  And said 'What a sharp bug am I.'"

Violet made a curtsy when she finished, but Mother Mouse was shaking her head. "I think it was Jack Horner who had the Christmas pie," Mother Mouse said.

"Of course, of course," said Father Mouse. "It was Jack Horner to be sure. Why, it's my favorite verse." He recited:

> *"Little Jack Horner*
> *Sat in the corner*
> *Eating his Christmas pie,*
> *He had a banana*
> *Tied in his bandanna*
> *But nobody ever knew why."*

"That still doesn't sound quite right," Mother Mouse said.

"It doesn't?" said Father Mouse with some surprise. "Why, it must be right—it's my favorite verse."

"*Polly put the pudding on,*" sang Baby Mouse, "*Polly put the pudding on—*"

"That's all wrong!" Violet scolded again.

"*Hey diddle diddle,*" said Baby Mouse, "*The*

*flute and the fiddle, the drum jumped over the
moon . . ."*

"Now that's a nice rhyme," said Father
Mouse. "What comes next?"

But Baby Mouse could not remember what
came next.

"Never mind, I have one," said Mother
Mouse.

> *"Doctor Foster went to Gloster*
> *On a winter's day.*
> *He stepped in the snows*
> *Up to his nose,*
> *And quickly melted away."*

Everyone clapped his paws together when
he heard this lovely verse, and Mother Mouse
blushed modestly.

Then the mice ate the good oatmeal cookie
and the soft sweet purple grape. It was a very
fine party, and they did not feel so sad or homesick.

"Now," said Father Mouse, "we are going
to play dressing-up."

32

Everyone liked that, and each tried to find something that would be the best costume of all.

Violet covered herself from head to foot with a white rag and said, "I am a ghost . . ."

All that showed was her tail as she ran across the floor.

"I want to be a ghost, too," said Baby Mouse. He got under a rag and ran all around bumping into things because he could not see where he was going.

Mother Mouse found an old feather duster in one corner of the cellar. She pulled out three feathers and made them into a fan by holding them close together in one small brown paw. Then she said, "I am a fine lady," and she fanned herself elegantly with the feathers from the duster.

Father Mouse found an old shoelace lying under the handyman's tool bench. He wound the shoelace around his stomach three times and tied a bow.

"Look at me," Father Mouse called to everyone. "I am dressed as a shoe."

5

Mother Mouse Explores

The next afternoon Mother Mouse decided that she would go upstairs and see what this strange house was like. She knew that the twenty-eight little girls were at school, and she had not heard much activity except someone walking across the kitchen floor now and then. Father Mouse was still out looking for Frederick, and Baby Mouse and Violet had fallen asleep after chasing each other around the paint cans until they were dizzy. It seemed a good time to explore. Mother Mouse covered up her children with extra rag scraps, so nothing showed but the tips of their noses. Then she went up the cellar steps and looked through the door.

The large sunny kitchen spread before her. The only person there was Cook, stirring something in a big bowl. She was making chocolate cookies for the little girls to eat when they came home from school. They were always hungry. That is the way children are. The little girls were always so hungry, it was a wonder to Cook that they ever got home from school at all without falling by the wayside weak with starvation.

After a short while, Cook put the cookies into the oven and went into the pantry to get the potatoes to peel for supper. She kept her eye on the clock as she worked, for it would soon be time to fix the afternoon tea tray. While Cook was in the pantry, Mother Mouse went very quietly across the kitchen floor and through the door that led to the dining room. There stretched the long dining-room table, set with twenty-eight little forks and knives and spoons. In the middle of the table was a large empty glass fruit bowl.

There was no one in sight.

Sunshine streamed through the windows and sparkled on the glass bowl. Mother Mouse went through the dining room, keeping close to the dark varnished molding at the bottom of the walls. The dining-room wallpaper was pale ivory with gold stripes—she could not help but notice how pretty it was.

Mother Mouse went to a door at the side of the dining room. Beyond the door was a large, long hall and a stairway going up to the next floor. Mother Mouse could see several doors. She was sure that one door, at the farthest end of the hall, was the front door. It was the biggest one of all, and beside it was a bench and a wooden hat rack and a forgotten umbrella stuck into the corner. At the sides of the door were tall narrow windows covered with white lace curtains.

Across from the dining room, the door to another room stood open. It was the only door that was open, and Mother Mouse waited until she was sure no one was looking, then she ran across the hall toward that open door. The hall was wide and the floor was brightly polished. Mother Mouse did not like running across such a wide, bright, open space. She was glad when she was safely across the hall, and she crouched behind a large potted fern and peeked through the open doorway.

The room was the parlor. Miss Lavender and Miss Plum, the two ladies who were in charge of The Good Day, were sitting together on the sofa, mending. They did not care much for this task and so the mending was always getting behind. Now it was terribly, terribly behind, and they had given up everything else for the day but the mending. (Miss Lavender thought it would be nice if they could finish in time to play some music. Miss Plum would play the piano and Miss Lavender would play her violin. But there was so much mending, it didn't seem likely they would get to anything else.)

Miss Plum sat very straight; thin as a pencil, straight as a ruler, as clean and neat as a fresh piece of paper or a brand-new school book or a pair of polished shoes. Her grayish hair was twisted into a bun on the top of her head, and she had her extra needle stuck onto the front of her dress, so it would be ready if she needed it.

Miss Lavender was not as thin as a pencil. She was as plump as a dish of pudding, as pretty as velvet bows and valentines, and as round as an orange. Even her gold-rimmed spectacles were round. Her dress was ruffly and flouncy, and below the last ruffle her short plump legs were crossed demurely at the ankles. "You can tell a true lady by the way she crosses her ankles," Miss Lavender always told the twenty-eight little girls.

Miss Lavender's hair was a lovely snowy white, and she had it arranged in a hundred soft white curls on the top of her head. Or at least it looked like about a hundred to Mother Mouse.

Mother Mouse watched the ladies sewing. Then she looked around the rest of the room.

There was a windowseat by the windows looking out toward the street. There was a small upright piano with music on the music rack and a rather worn blue cushion on the piano stool. The cushion had a tassel about three inches long, that trailed down from it. Mother Mouse thought it was the most beautiful cushion she had ever seen.

There was a fireplace and a clock ticking away on the mantel above. There were five tiny china figures lined up beside the clock—figures of china cats—and Mother Mouse stared at them boldly. China cats didn't scare her. They couldn't even move.

There was also a pink seashell on the mantelpiece, and a small book with a blue velvet cover and gold letters: *Never-ending Stories.*

"Oh—oh," said Miss Plum, who happened to look up at the clock on the mantel just then. "It's nearly three o'clock, Miss Lavender."

Miss Lavender looked extremely distressed to hear this. She took everything she was sewing and crammed it down into her sewing basket and tried to get the lid on. The basket was too full by a long, long way, and the lid kept bouncing up again as fast as she pushed it down.

Miss Plum said, "Here," and gave Miss Lavender all the things she was mending. Then Miss Plum got up and began to hurry around the room straightening things. Miss Lavender tried to get all of Miss Plum's mending into the basket, too, and both ladies were hard at work when there came a knock at the front door. A terrible knock that shook the whole door.

Mother Mouse jumped to hear this loud, unexpected sound. Miss Plum stopped her work. There was no time to do anything else to make the room tidy. But it did not look too bad—except for the sewing basket, which was bulging and popping open.

"Mr. Not So Much is here," Miss Plum said. She opened a closet door and pushed the sewing basket into the closet beside Miss Lavender's violin case.

Mother Mouse heard the ladies' footsteps coming out of the parlor. Right past the potted fern they came: Miss Plum very erect and trying to look calm; Miss Lavender wringing her hands and flouncing her ruffles and sighing to herself. Before they reached the door another mighty knock fell upon it, and Mother Mouse squeezed back behind the potted fern as far as she could squeeze.

6

Mr. Not So Much

The caller at the door was indeed Mr. Not So Much, as Miss Plum had said. He was a member of the Board of Directors of The Good Day, and it was his duty to come calling once a month to see how things were getting along. He had been arriving in this same way for twenty years. Miss Lavender could not keep track of how long Mr. Not So Much had been coming, but Miss Plum said it was twenty years. Miss Plum always knew best about everything, and Miss Lavender always agreed with what Miss Plum said.

42

Mr. Not So Much was very tall and thin. He always wore black suits and black hats and a watch with a long heavy chain. When he came for his visits he told Cook not to put so much sugar in the cookies. He told Miss Lavender not to put so much wood on the fire. He told Miss Plum not to spend so much money for this and not so much money for that. He always seemed surprised to see that The Good Day was still running, even with such wasteful ways. Then he would put on his hat and go away for another month.

Mother Mouse watched timidly from behind the fern as Mr. Not So Much came into the parlor with Miss Lavender and Miss Plum. He had barely had time to take off his coat and hat, when Cook entered with a tray of tea-things. Mr. Not So Much looked at the tea tray glumly.

Miss Plum poured a cup of tea for Mr. Not So Much, and when the cup was nearly full, he said, "Not so much tea." Miss Plum put in a lump of sugar and he said, "Not so much sugar." Miss Lavender squeezed in a twist of lemon and he said, "Not so much lemon."

Then Miss Plum handed him the cup and Mr. Not So Much tasted his tea.

Cook was returning to the kitchen, and Mother Mouse held her breath behind the potted fern as Cook's sturdy shoes clumped by. One lace had come untied, and Cook stopped to tie it up again. She was almost on top of poor Mother Mouse. But she did not see Mother Mouse, and when her shoe was tied Cook straightened up and went on her way.

Mr. Not So Much set down his cup and reached for a cake.

"Not so much frosting on these cakes," he said as he ate. "Waste not, want not, ladies; waste not, want not."

"Waste not, want not," Miss Plum agreed.

"Yes, indeed," said Miss Lavender.

"A fool and his money are soon parted," said Mr. Not So Much.

"Oh, how true," Miss Plum agreed.

"How true, indeed," said Miss Lavender. But she thought the cakes tasted just perfect the way they were.

Just then the clock struck three, and Mother Mouse skittered as fast as she could across the big bare polished floor of the hallway. Already she had been gone too long from her children. Across the dining room she ran, boldly, right under the middle of the table. At the kitchen door she paused only long enough to be sure the way was safe. Cook was at the sink peeling the potatoes for supper; her back was turned to Mother Mouse. Mother Mouse hurried across the kitchen floor and through the half-opened cellar door and down into the dark safety of the cellar.

Under the stairs Violet and Baby Mouse were just beginning to wake up from their naps. They were wondering where their mama was, and Baby Mouse had already begun to cry a little about it, so she was back just in time.

Upstairs in the parlor Mr. Not So Much finished his tea. He began going over the monthly bills with Miss Lavender and Miss Plum. Every few minutes, through the floor, Mother Mouse could hear him saying ". . . not

so much . . . not so much," although his voice
was faint and far away. ". . . waste not, want
not, ladies . . . waste not, want not . . ."

Mother Mouse was glad to be safely back
in the cellar, but then a dreadful thing happened. The handyman came down the steps
from the yard and took his rake and work
gloves from the corner where he kept his paint
cans and tools. Mother Mouse and her children
kept very still in the rags in the bushel basket.
Soon the handyman went up the stairs again.
He had left the slanting wooden door propped
wide open, and now as he went out he closed it
behind him, but as he did so he caught sight of
the stone that kept one corner from closing
completely. He kicked the stone away with his
heavy shoe, and the door came down tight to
the ground. Now there was no way for Father
Mouse to get back in when he did return.

Mother Mouse did not say anything to Violet and Baby Mouse, for she did not want to
worry them. But as they played in a puddle of
water that had splashed out by the laundry
tubs, Mother Mouse ran back and forth by that

door, sniffing and scratching and poking her nose at it to see if she could not, after all, find some tiny hole or crack through which Father Mouse could crawl. She could find nothing bigger than a pinpoint of light along one side, no space at all for even a very small mouse to get through. At last Mother Mouse gave up, and crept to the sill of one of the basement windows. The afternoon had grown dark and chilly. She could see out across the front lawn to the black iron gate and the Square beyond. Sadly she watched for Father Mouse.

Suddenly she heard a wild and ferocious barking and saw a large black dog tearing along the street. Then she saw that Father Mouse himself was running just far enough ahead of the dog to keep out of its jaws.

Poor Father Mouse. Where, oh, where was he to go!

Through the black iron fence flew Father Mouse, his feet hardly touching the ground. The dog could not follow him through the fence, but Father Mouse was not taking any chances. His feet hardly touched the ground as

he covered the yard—only to find the cellar door tightly closed.

At the fence the great dog had risen on his hind legs and poked his huge head through the rails, barking as savagely as ever. To Father Mouse the barks seemed practically upon him. With one last terrified look at the dog straining at the fence, Father Mouse raced on around the house and up to the first place he came to—the back door. Cook had left the door open a few inches to cool the kitchen, where chocolate cookies were baking and the potatoes for supper were peeled and ready to put in the oven.

In through the kitchen door went Father Mouse, while the handyman, roused by all the noise, came from his raking at the other side of the house and chased off the dog.

"Go on there! What are you making all that racket for?" he called, waving his rake at the dog. "Off with you—off with you—"

Cook did not see Father Mouse as he came rushing into her kitchen, and Father Mouse was so flustered and breathless and confused that he kept right on running, straight through the kitchen, straight through the dining room, straight into the hallway. And so it was that he nearly collided with Mr. Not So Much, just that moment appearing out of the parlor, his hat raised to clap on his head, his visit over for the month.

"There is a mouse here!" Mr. Not So Much thundered in his fearsome voice. He towered above Father Mouse—and then poor frightened Father Mouse truly did not know which way to turn.

7

There Is a Mouse Here

"There is a mouse here!" Mr. Not So Much said again, and Father Mouse came to his senses and turned and rushed back the way he had come. Back across the hall, into the dining room, toward the kitchen. His little heart was hammering in his little chest and his tiny feet had never gone so fast. His tail streamed out behind him.

Miss Plum and Miss Lavender came out of the parlor to see what Mr. Not So Much was shouting about. But Mr. Not So Much did not wait for them. He was striding through the din-

51

ing room, in pursuit of the mouse. At the kitchen door Mr. Not So Much said, "There is a mouse here. I just saw it running through the hall."

At the word "mouse," Cook froze as stiff as a board. The big spoon she had been taking out of a kitchen drawer clattered from her hand down to the floor.

Miss Plum and Miss Lavender arrived behind Mr. Not So Much at the kitchen door in time to hear what he said.

"*A mouse?*" Miss Plum exclaimed indignantly. "We do not have any mice here."

"No, of course not," Miss Lavender looked somewhat confused, but she always agreed with things Miss Plum said. "Of course we do not have any mice here."

"There is a mouse here now," Mr. Not So Much said. "I just saw it. It came right through the dining room, through this door, into this kitchen. Didn't you see it?" he asked Cook.

But it did no good to talk to Cook. She was frozen stiff, and her eyes were as round as the plates on the rack above the kitchen table. Mr.

Not So Much looked more startled to see Cook than he had been to see the mouse. He leaned forward the peered at her closely, but she only stared back from her wide, frightened, frozen eyes.

"Now, there is nothing to be afraid of," Miss Plum said gently to Cook. She gave Mr. Not So Much a very reproving look, scolding him for having frightened poor Cook so badly. "We have never had mice in this house, and we do not have any now," she said.

Mr. Not So Much did not seem to know whether to say any more about the mouse or not. He had not known poor Cook would be so frightened.

Miss Lavender peeked timidly around Miss Plum's shoulder. "Did—I mean—did you really think you saw—I mean—I mean—a mouse?" She whispered the last few words, but Cook heard and jerked stiffly.

"Yes, I did," said Mr. Not So Much firmly. What was true was true. He had seen a mouse and there was no use saying now that he hadn't. Ladies always made such a fuss about

such simple things. He was sure he would never understand them.

Just then the front door burst open and twenty-eight little girls came rushing in from school, chattering and giggling and dropping school books here and there along the way as they came directly to the kitchen to see what good things Cook had fixed for them to eat.

But the girls began to slow down and stop chattering and giggling when they saw Miss Lavender and Miss Plum and Mr. Not So Much—and poor Cook frozen stiff as a board.

"What's the matter?" one of the little girls asked. Her name was Mary. She had a round face and red hair and freckles. Beside her were her special friends, Tatty and Little Ann, and behind them all the other girls crowded for-

ward to look into the kitchen to see what was happening.

Before Miss Plum had a chance to warn Miss Lavender not to startle the girls, Miss Lavender blurted out, "Mr. Not So Much has seen a mouse—"

"A mouse! A mouse!" The words ran back through the clusters of girls to the very last one of all, a tall vain girl named Elsie May, who thought she was the best girl of all. She wrinkled up her nose with distaste and looked about along the floor to be sure that the mouse was not near her.

By that time Father Mouse had long since been safely down in the cellar. Just before Mr. Not So Much reached the kitchen door, Father Mouse had slipped through the door that led downstairs to the cellar. He was at that very moment in the farthest part of the bushel basket, with Mother Mouse and Violet and Baby Mouse, all clinging together and shaking under the scraps.

All the girls began to jump up and down

and say, "We want to see the mouse, we want to see the mouse, we want to see the mouse . . ."

"Not so much noise," Mr. Not So Much roared, and all the little girls got very quiet right away.

Cook, still rigid with fright, did not even seem to be breathing. Miss Plum looked at her with some concern. "We do not have a mouse here," Miss Plum said, as loudly as she could speak and still be ladylike. ("No shouting" was one of Miss Plum's rules for the girls, and she tried to set them a good example. But she was beginning to feel very much like shouting herself.) "We do not have any mice here," she continued. "We have never had mice in this house and we do not have any now. What a thing to say! Mice on our premises!"

"Where are the premises?" Little Ann asked Mary, but Mary said she did not know.

Mr. Not So Much took one more look at Cook, standing stiff with eyes bulging; at the twenty-eight staring little girls; at Miss Plum's outraged expression and Miss Lavender's fluttery dismay—and he was certainly sorry that he had ever said anything about the mouse in the first place.

"Miss Plum is right, you know," Miss Lavender said, holding her snowy white pile of curls as high as she could. "We do not have mice, Mr. Not So Much."

Mr. Not So Much put on his hat and said, "Ladies, you may be right."

And then he got out of there as quickly as he could. The little girls fell away to either side as he came out of the kitchen, but as soon as the front door closed behind him they began to clamor again.

"Isn't there any mouse?"

"Can't we see the mouse?"

"Where's the mouse?"

Miss Lavender had to hurry them all away from the kitchen so that Miss Plum could comfort Cook.

"How many mice have you ever seen here, Cook?" Miss Plum said.

"None," Cook admitted, when she got her voice back again.

"Do you think I would let mice get into this house?"

"No, I suppose—not," Cook answered. She was still very much upset by what Mr. Not So Much had said. Even after Miss Plum helped her look carefully around the kitchen, behind everything and under everything and into every cupboard, so she could see for herself there was no mouse there—even then Cook was still not completely convinced.

"I will even go into the cellar and look there, to prove to you that we do not have any mice here," Miss Plum said.

The mouse family heard Miss Plum's steps. The little mice were under the stairs, and her steps were very close to them. Each creaking board sounded right in their ears. When she had come down the steps, she walked around the cellar, her hands folded carefully in front of her, her chin up quite proudly. Mice, indeed! To think of such a thing! Miss Plum sniffed disdainfully. When she had looked all around the cellar, Miss Plum went back upstairs to the kitchen.

"There is no mouse in that cellar, Cook," she said. And Cook felt a little better after that.

But, nevertheless, it was a great chore for her to get the supper that night, for she kept dropping spoons and things and looking over her shoulder to be sure there was no mouse watching her.

8

The Top of the Window

Now the mouse family had to be very quiet. More quiet than ever before. They slept badly that night, dreaming they heard footsteps coming down the cellar stairs again; and they were all awake long before daylight, hunched on their rag scraps and listening for sounds in the house above.

As it grew light outside, Father Mouse began to hunt about along the cellar walls and windowsills for a place where he might go in and out, now that the stone from the door had been removed. In their cellar at home there was

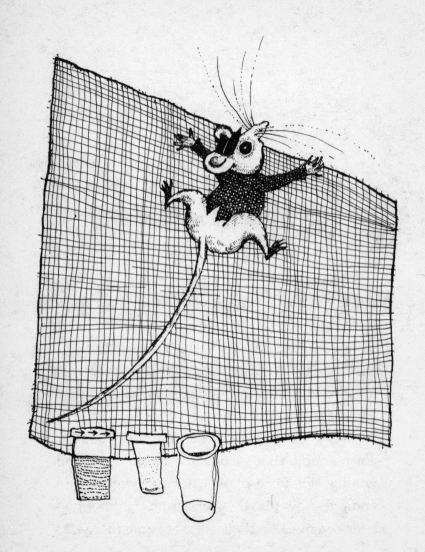

a hole under a board in the wall. But there was nothing like that in this cellar. Father Mouse had almost given up, when he found a window at the back of the cellar which had been left open a tiny bit at the top. He could reach the opening from a shelf that was on the wall beside the window. He went back under the stairs and reported what he had found to Mother Mouse. "Now I must be on my way again, looking for Frederick," he said to her.

Mother Mouse and Violet and Baby Mouse watched Father Mouse go along the shelf and jump to the top of the window. They saw him drop down to the ground on the other side. He waved back at them through the window, and then he was off across the yard.

At last Violet and Baby Mouse began to play, and Mother Mouse said, "Remember, we must be extra quiet now, or someone will come downstairs looking for us again."

So the mouse children played very quietly all that day. But even so, after school that afternoon some little girls came down into the cellar, prowling around and looking to see if they could find a mouse.

"If Mr. Not So Much said he saw one, I'll bet he did," said the little girl named Tatty. Her dark hair fell in her eyes and her stockings wrinkled around her legs for she never remembered to keep them pulled up smooth and tight. She was nearly eight years old, and she wished that she would find a sweet little mouse. She had never seen a real live mouse, only pictures in storybooks. And she had brought some bread crumbs in her pocket, in case she found a mouse.

With Tatty came Mary, the girl with red hair. She was older than Tatty by a whole year and a half, and she had seen real live mice once when a boy in her room at school brought his pet white mice to show the class. Mary thought all mice were white, and she was looking for a plump white mouse with a pink nose.

With Tatty and Mary was Little Ann. She was the very smallest of all the girls in The Good Day. She was only five years old, and she was not helping to look for the mouse very

much. She was just playing and poking into things and examining the handyman's tools which she found lying around. She thought the cellar was a very exciting place and she soon forgot all about the mouse.

But Tatty and Mary looked. They looked under the wheelbarrow and behind the garden tools. They looked behind the old newspapers piled up waiting for the junkman to take away. They looked behind some empty boxes in one corner. And under the laundry tubs. And inside the clothespin basket.

Cook came to the top of the stairs—no closer—and called down, "Have you found anything?"

Cook wanted to believe Miss Plum, that there had never been any mice in that house and there weren't any now; but sometimes she felt sure there was a mouse around *some*where, watching her. Sometimes she was sure she would see a mouse, any moment, running across her clean kitchen floor.

Finally the little girls went back upstairs and the kitchen door closed. Tatty took her bread crumbs with her and ate them herself. Then the cellar was dark again. Mother Mouse and Violet and Baby Mouse crept out of the bushel basket and waited in a forlorn and silent row for Father Mouse to come home. Upstairs they could hear Miss Lavender and Miss Plum playing the violin and piano. Sweetly and softly the music came down to the little brown mice as they waited.

But that afternoon Father Mouse did not come back. It grew later and later. It was finally dark outside and everyone had gone to bed in the house, and still he did not come. There was no supper for Violet or Baby Mouse or Mother Mouse, and at last Mother Mouse said they must all go to bed.

"Where is Father?" Violet wanted to know.

"He will be along soon. Now you go to sleep," Mother Mouse said.

When Violet and Baby Mouse were asleep, Mother Mouse crept out of the bushel basket and went to sit by the cellar window again. She was not at all sure that Father Mouse would be along soon. She had said that so the children would not worry. But Mother Mouse knew that Father Mouse would not stay away so long unless something had happened that would keep him from getting back to them.

Now Frederick and Father Mouse were both gone. Mother Mouse stared into the dark night and the dark street beyond the cellar window. She did not cry one tear. She hunched up into a ball to keep warm, and she waited by the window all the whole night long.

But Father Mouse did not come back.

9

Tatty

The next day was the worst of all. More little girls came down to the cellar looking to see if they could find a mouse. They laughed and made noise, running around everywhere. When they got tired of looking for a mouse they rolled the wheelbarrow around and swept the floor with an old broom they found, and then they began to play hide-and-seek.

Father Mouse still had not returned. Mother Mouse and Violet and Baby Mouse went to the farthest-back spot they could get to under the stairs. They were not even in the bushel basket anymore, but crouched behind it, pressing their brown furry backs against the wall. Baby Mouse was trembling all over and Violet closed her eyes tight, put her head in her paws, and would not look.

When the girls began to play hide-and-seek, Little Ann came under the stairs to hide. She sat down in the bushel basket. *Oh,* thought Mother Mouse, *we would all have been sat upon if we had stayed there!* Little Ann waited until another girl found her and dragged her out from under the stairs, basket and all.

"Here, here, you youngsters," the handyman called, coming in from the yard where he had been trimming the hedges. "You put that basket back and get on out of here now. Miss Plum doesn't let you play down here. Scat— scat—"

The girls pushed the basket back and ran away laughing and shouting up the stairs into the yard. There they scattered like leaves blown by the wind, and the mouse family could hear them crying: "You're it—" "I tagged you—"

"Can't catch me, can't catch me—" Then the handyman closed down the slanting wooden door again, and all was quiet.

"This will never do," said Mother Mouse. "Every day more people are coming down into this cellar."

"Are we going home?" asked Violet.

Mother Mouse did not answer at once. Then she said, "No. We will wait for your father. And Frederick."

The three mice were silent for a few minutes, each thinking his own thoughts— wondering where Father Mouse and Frederick were, and when they would see them again.

At last Mother Mouse said, "We musn't sit here counting our troubles. Let's have some songs and rhymes."

"All right," said Violet, but before she could begin, Baby Mouse said: *"Mary had a little duck, its feathers white as snow . . ."*

"That's not right at all," Violet said with a sniff.

"Are you sure?" asked Baby Mouse. It

seemed that he never got his verses quite right.

"Yes, of course I'm sure," said Violet.

"Mary had a little cat, its whiskers white as snow. Everyone knows that."

"A cat?" said Baby Mouse. "I don't think I like that verse then. Say another, Violet."

Violet said:

> *"Mary, Mary, quite contrary*
> *How does your schoolwork go?*
> *Arithmetic and geography*
> *And spelling words all in a row."*

Almost before she was finished, Baby Mouse had thought of another rhyme himself.

> *"The king was in the countinghouse*
> *Standing on his nose,*
> *The queen was in the parlor*
> *Watering her rose."*

"Please stop," Violet begged.

But before Violet could say any more,

Mother Mouse said, "Now it's my turn." And
she began:

> *"Jack Sprat could eat no tacks*
> *His wife could eat no nails,*
> *And so between them both, you see,*
> *They ate the plates and pails."*

But it was not the same without Father
Mouse. They all wished he were there to say
his favorite verse.

> *Little Jack Horner*
> *Sat in the corner*
> *Eating his Christmas pie,*
> *He had a banana*
> *Tied in his bandanna*
> *But nobody ever knew why . . .*

It grew darker and darker. Night was coming. Again there was no supper for Violet and
Baby Mouse and Mother Mouse. It was better
to be hungry and stay together, Mother Mouse

thought. What if she went to the kitchen looking for food and something happened to her? What would become of Violet and Baby Mouse *then*. So she did not go to find any food.

Upstairs everything grew quiet at last, as everyone went to bed. When Violet and Baby Mouse were asleep, too, Mother Mouse settled herself down all alone by the window.

How long should she wait, she wondered. What if Father Mouse did not come back at all? Could she ever find her way across the city back home without him? Mother Mouse shivered, huddled in the darkness alone. Now all her family was separated. They were not together anymore. And all she had wanted was to keep her family together, safe, where she could watch after them and take care of them all. That is the way mothers are. She knew the city was full of strange dogs and cats; it was full of fast cars rushing along with horns blowing and wheels screeching; it was full of strange children, and who knew how many other things dangerous to little mice like Frederick and Father Mouse.

All the cold, lonesome night Mother Mouse sat by the cellar window. She was waiting for Father Mouse to come back. And she did not cry one tear.

Then just at daylight, before Mother Mouse heard any sounds of Cook making breakfast in the kitchen above, the door in the kitchen opened very quietly and a little girl came down the cellar stairs, tiptoeing on small bare feet. Mother Mouse felt panicky because she was so far from Violet and Baby Mouse. They were sleeping in the bushel basket, and here she was way across the cellar in plain view on the windowsill. She did not dare move, and the little girl did not see her, for the cellar was shadowy and dim in the early morning light.

"Here mousy, mousy, mousy," said the little girl. It was Tatty. She had gotten up before anyone else was awake. She had saved a small piece of bread from her supper the night before, and she sat on the stairs crumbling it and tossing the crumbs down the steps to a bare spot on the cellar floor.

"Here mousy, mousy," she called again softly.

Mother Mouse watched with considerable surprise. She had never seen anyone doing anything like this before. Violet and Baby Mouse slept on undisturbed. Tatty was calling so softly that she did not even waken them. Mother Mouse sat as still as the china cats she had seen on the mantelpiece in the parlor. She did not move a whisker or even the tip of her tail.

By and by the bread was all broken into crumbs. Quite a delicious-looking pile lay on the floor at the bottom of the stairs. And then at last, with a sigh, Tatty stood up and went back up the stairs to the kitchen. Mother Mouse did not move right away. She wanted to be sure that it was safe. She could not hear much, for Tatty was tiptoeing as secretly as she could back through the house and upstairs to her bed. She did not want anyone to know she was up so early.

When everything had been quiet for a while, Mother Mouse came down from the windowsill and tasted the bread crumbs. They were real bread crumbs all right; very fresh and tasty. Mother Mouse hurried to wake up Violet and Baby Mouse, who were sleepy, but not too sleepy to eat. It had been two days since they had had any food.

10

The Dark Pantry

Father Mouse had not come back because he was trapped in a strange house several blocks away from Butterfield Square. He had scampered into a pantry, looking for Frederick, and before he could scamper out again someone had closed the pantry door. Then it was very dark. There was only one tiny window and it had a heavy curtain over it; when night-time came, the darkness was like a wall closing in around poor Father Mouse.

Heartbroken, he sat all night by the closed door. Mother Mouse would be so worried, he thought. And how could he ever find Frederick if he himself was trapped in a pantry?

At last morning came, but Father Mouse did not hear any sounds in the rooms on the other side of the pantry door. All day he waited and listened and hoped that someone would come and open the door. At last, at nightfall, he did hear some voices, and footsteps coming in the back door. The people were home from wherever they had been all day—but they did not open the pantry door that night, and soon the house grew very still again.

"Oh, they've gone to bed," Father Mouse said sadly to himself. The pantry was full of food, and he ate a small piece of apple to keep up his strength, but he did not have much interest in the food in view of all his other worries. I would rather starve, he thought, and be with my family!

Then another lonely night passed in the dark pantry, with not even a stray spider to talk to. There was nothing there but food . . . and one small brown mouse.

But at last, after Father Mouse had been

trapped one night and one day and another night, a woman opened the door. She came into the pantry, and began to look among the cereal boxes on the back shelf. Father Mouse wasted no time making a dash from the pantry across the kitchen to the back door. It was an old screen door that did not close all the way, and in a moment Father Mouse was out into the alley, blinking in the bright sunshine and hardly able to realize his good fortune.

Almost before he could get his eyes accustomed to the brightness after so long a time in the dark pantry, good fortune appeared again— in the form of a boy carrying a small wire cage along the alley.

In the cage was Frederick Mouse.

11

The Mouse in the Cage

It really was Frederick! Father Mouse rubbed his eyes and gaped in astonishment, and the boy went on up the alley and turned the corner and walked off down the street. Father Mouse came to life and raced after the boy, calling *"Fred-er-ick! Fred-er-ick!"* as loudly as he could.

"Father! Father!" Frederick called back, rushing frantically from one end of his tiny cage to the other. But it only sounded like squeaking to the boy.

"Stop your squeaking," he said to his mouse. "Stop scattering your straw."

"*Fred-er-ick! Fred-er-ick!*" Father Mouse kept calling as he ran along behind the boy.

"*Father! Father!*" Frederick called back, exhausting himself by one mad whirl after another against the sides of the cage.

A group of boys sat on the front steps of one of the houses along the street, and the boy carrying the mouse cage went up the walk toward that house. Father Mouse fell behind and waited by a bush. Little by little, as the boys talked, he squirmed his way through the grass toward the steps of the house. He was not going to lose sight of Frederick again after finding him at last.

"Hi, Donny. What have you got in the cage?" one of the boys asked, getting up from his seat on the steps.

"Hey," another said, "isn't that your pet mouse?"

The boy carrying the cage set it down on the bottom step and stood back proudly so everyone could have a good look. The boys crowded around the cage. Frederick rolled himself up in a ball and closed his eyes. It frightened him to see so many boys staring at him. Their faces looked very big, so close to the cage. Where was Father Mouse—oh, where had he gone? Shivering, frightened, and miserable, Frederick huddled in his straw.

"I'm going to sell him," said the boy named Donny.

"Sell your mouse?" the others all asked. Most of them looked rather longingly at the cage.

"Why?" one of the boys asked. He stuck his finger through the tiny wires and wiggled it at the ball of mouse fur in the corner.

"I'm selling everything I can," Donny said. "I'm saving for a new bicycle."

The other boys thought about this, and one said quickly, "Gee, I don't have any money, but I'll trade you my baseball mitt. It's practically as good as new."

Someone laughed to hear *this;* but the owner of the mouse only shook his head. "I want money," he said.

"I'll give you my leather marble-pouch—the one my aunt brought me from her trip to Alaska," another boy shouted eagerly. "There are twenty marbles, too."

"No good," said Donny. "I want money, you guys. How can I get a new bike with baseball mitts and marble-bags?"

"How much money do you think it's worth?" another boy asked.

"What'll you give me?" Donny said.

Father Mouse was quite close to the boys by this time. He was horrified to hear his own Frederick talked about like a toy in a shop. He tried to see Frederick but the boys were crowded around the cage.

"I'll give you a dime for it, Donny," a boy said.

"A dime?" Donny sounded disgusted. "A dime?"

"I'll give you fifteen cents," another boy said.

"Fifteen cents?" said Donny. "Aw, you guys are wasting my time."

"What do you think we are, millionaires?"

Before Donny could answer that, another boy asked, "Does the cage go with it, Donny?"

"Sure," Donny said. "The cage goes, too. The cage is worth fifteen cents even without the mouse."

Everyone looked at the cage. "Hey," one boy said, "are you sure that mouse is still alive?"

Father Mouse's heart almost stopped beating when he heard this. What did the boy mean? Oh, why didn't they move out of the way so he could see Frederick.

"Yeah," another boy said. "He's not moving."

"Of course he's alive," Donny said. "He's just scared because you're making such a racket." He jiggled the cage, and Frederick swished his tail and turned his head to see what was happening now.

"Yeah, I guess he's alive all right," someone said.

Father Mouse felt weak with relief. He crouched in the grass, trying to think of how he could rescue Frederick, and the boys went on arguing among themselves about how much the mouse and the cage were worth.

"Come on," said Donny, growing more eager as the boys offered more money. "Thirty cents—Jacky says thirty cents. Who'll bid thirty-five? Who'll bid thirty-five? Come on, you guys. Who'll make it thirty-five?"

Money, money, money, Father Mouse thought to himself. Everything is money, money, money these days. Even my own dear Frederick.

But a daring plan was forming in his mind.

"Thirty-five cents," said one of the boys at last. He was the boy with the leather pouch from Alaska, and he swung the pouch back and forth by its drawstring as he spoke.

Father Mouse took a deep breath and ran into the middle of the group of boys.

"Frederick, Frederick," he called, *"get ready—get ready to go—"*

"Hey!" the boys cried, staring down with amazement at the brown mouse who had run suddenly into their midst.

"Hey—catch it, catch it—" they called to

each other. Father Mouse pretended to run first this way and then that, but he was not really trying to get away, and after dodging out of reach a few times he let the boy named Donny close his hand around him. Oh, what a horrible, horrible feeling—to be held so tight in the strange boy's hand, which was none too clean!

"Quick—open the cage door for me," Donny commanded. He could hardly believe his good luck. Now he would have two mice to sell.

"Get ready, Frederick," Father Mouse screamed at the top of his voice.

Father Mouse's cry only sounded like squeaking to the boys, and they hardly noticed that Frederick had uncurled himself and was watching the cage door with his bright black eyes. The boys were all watching Donny and Father Mouse. Frederick moved closer toward the door as one of the boys fumbled with the unfamiliar catch. Every muscle in Frederick's body was tense for a spring right through that door as soon as his chance came.

Father Mouse had grown very still in the boy's hand.

"There," said the boy as the cage door opened.

But just as the door opened wide, Father Mouse wriggled as hard as he could, scratched with his tiny feet, and sank his teeth into Donny's hard thumb. The little mouse could not really scratch or bite very hard, but the boy was so startled at the sudden, unexpected movement that he dropped Father Mouse with a cry of surprise.

Out flew Frederick through the open cage door, and away raced the two mice across the grass and down the street as fast as their legs would carry them. The boys came running after with so much shouting that everyone along the street stopped to stare at them—and the bag from Alaska dropped and fell open and marbles rolled everywhere—*plink, plink, plink, plink.*

12

Going Home

When Mother Mouse saw Father Mouse and Frederick coming along Butterfield Square, two tiny tears came into her eyes. The tears got fuller and fuller and bigger and bigger, and rolled down her face. She moved away from the windowsill to allow Father Mouse and Frederick room to jump down from the opening at the top of the window. They came over the window top, puffing and panting and wildly thrilled by their escape.

"Frederick!" sobbed Mother Mouse, and be-

gan to cover her long-lost child with kisses. The
tears glistened on her furry brown face.

"Why are you crying now?" exclaimed Father Mouse. "Now everything is all right. We
have found Frederick and we can be on our
way home."

"I am crying because I am so happy," said

Mother Mouse. She tried to dry her tears with the end of her tail.

"No time for tears, no time for tears." Father Mouse was so excited he could hardly stand still.

"No time for tears," Frederick echoed. He could hardly stand still either. He was looking all around this strange cellar . . . but before he could ask how his family had come to be there, Violet and Baby Mouse came running from behind the paint cans where they had fallen asleep, and they began to kiss Frederick, too, and ask him a hundred questions.

"Little girls have been coming down here looking for us," Mother Mouse told Father Mouse.

"Then let us be on our way at once," Father Mouse said. "There is no reason to stay here any longer."

They took a farewell look around the cellar. Everything was just as they had found it. They had disturbed nothing. You would never know that a mouse family had ever been there.

They went out one by one through the

opening at the top of the window. They went across the yard and slipped out between the rails of the black iron fence. It was quite chilly. Winter would soon be here. They were glad to be going home. Glad they had Frederick safely back. Glad they would all soon be snug together on the old woolen sweater and the piece of red carpet in their very own cellar.

They ran along, very happy, keeping close together and near to the protection of bushes and fences so that no one would notice them. But there was hardly a soul to be seen along the Square that chilly afternoon, and the dry leaves rustling by the curb seemed to be saying, "Hurry home . . . winter is coming . . ."

Suddenly Father Mouse could not resist shouting out, he was so full of joy.

> *"Little Jack Horner*
> *Sat in the corner*
> *Eating his Christmas pie,"*

he called triumphantly. He had taken Frederick to the kitchen and lost him—and now he had found him and rescued him. He could not be silent!

As the mouse family reached the corner and turned off Butterfield Square toward their own home across the city, Father Mouse's voice grew fainter and fainter in the distance . . .

> *"He had a banana*
> *Tied in his bandanna*
> *But nobody*

ever
knew
why."

One day, not long after, Miss Plum made one last search for mice in the cellar to satisfy Cook.

"You must come down and see for yourself," she said to Cook. The twenty-eight little girls had come along to help Miss Plum, and they made room for Cook to come down the stairs into the cellar. Tatty wondered if anyone would notice the bread crumbs she had been sprinkling around here and there. Every day she tried to bring a few. No one—or no thing— ate them now, and they dried up into nothing. But once—once—she remembered, she had sat on the steps and called, "Here mousy, mousy, mousy," and tossed bread crumbs down to the cellar floor; and those bread crumbs had been gone when she came back later. All gone. Every crumb.

Cook came down from the kitchen reluctantly, very slowly, step by step. She kept a tight hold on the handrail with one hand, and a tight hold on the corner of her apron with the other. When Cook was down, everyone stood and stared around silently, but no one noticed the bread crumbs. There was not a sound in that whole cellar but the *drip-drip* of water from the faucet at the laundry tubs.

"There, you see," said Miss Plum, turning the faucet tighter so the water would stop dripping. "There are no mice here. There never have been mice in this house, and there never will be."

"Well," said Cook, "I'm glad to know that."

But Tatty only smiled to herself, as though she had a secret.

ABOUT THE AUTHOR

CAROL BEACH YORK is a writer with over forty outstanding juvenile and young adult books to her credit, including the popular Bantam titles *Remember Me When I Am Dead, I Will Make You Disappear, On That Dark Night, Miss Know It All,* and *Miss Know It All Returns.* Born and raised in Chicago, she began her career writing short stories and sold her first one to *Seventeen* magazine. Her first teen novel, a romance, *Sparrow Lake,* was published in 1962. Since then she has contributed many stories and articles to magazines in both the juvenile and adult markets, in addition to her activity as a novelist. She especially enjoys writing suspense stories. Ms. York lives in Chicago with her daughter, Diana.

☐ **DANNY, THE CHAMPION PONY** 15193/$1.95
by Suzette Winter

To Andrea Cummings, Danny is just another pony on her parents' huge estate. But to Janie Neely, who works around the stable, Danny is a dream—the handsomest pony she's ever seen. When Danny develops a limp Janie is determined to cure him. She believes that if you hold fast to your dreams they will come true.

Buy them at your local bookstore or use this handy coupon for ordering:

WITTY ADVENTURES BY
FLORENCE PARRY HEIDE books

Shop at home
for quality childrens books
and save money, too.

Now you can order books for the whole family from Bantam's latest listing of hundreds of titles including many fine children's books. *And* this special offer gives you an opportunity to purchase a Bantam book for only 50¢. Here's how:

By ordering any five books at the regular price per order, you can also choose any other single book listed (up to $4.95 value) for just 50¢. Some restrictions do apply, so for further details send for Bantam's listing of titles today.

Here are more of the "kid-pleasing" paperbacks that everyone loves.